Ladybird  Readers

Animal Colors

Series Editor: Sorrel Pitts
Written by Rachel Godfrey

LADYBIRD BOOKS

UK | USA | Canada | Ireland | Australia
India | New Zealand | South Africa

Ladybird Books is part of the Penguin Random House group of companies
whose addresses can be found at global.penguinrandomhouse.com.
www.penguin.co.uk   www.puffin.co.uk   www.ladybird.co.uk

First published 2019
001

Printed in China

A CIP catalogue record for this book is available from the British Library

ISBN: 978–0–241–35792–7

All correspondence to:
Ladybird Books
Penguin Random House Children's
80 Strand, London WC2R 0RL

Ladybird Readers

BBC earth

Animal Colors

Inspired by BBC Earth TV series and
developed with input from BBC Earth
natural history specialists

Contents

Picture words

frog

gecko

ibex

insect

rat

snow leopard

desert

fur

grasslands

jungle

mountains

rock

sand

snow

Animal colors

What colors are these animals?

This animal is brown, black, and white.

This animal is brown and green.

This animal is orange, brown, black, and pink.

This animal is yellow, brown, white, and black.

9

Color helps animals

Color helps some animals, because other animals cannot see them.

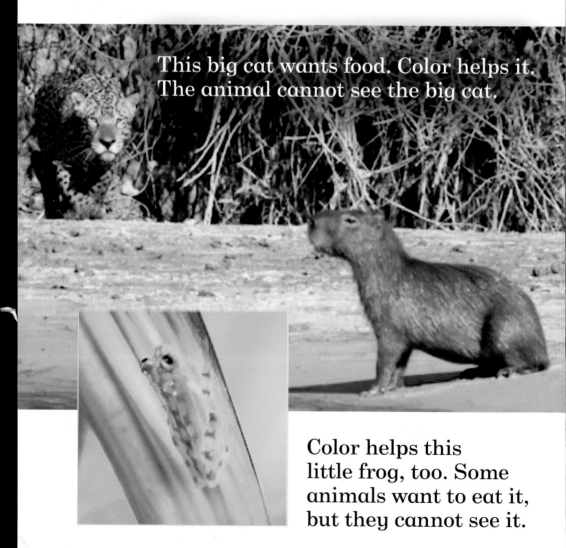

This big cat wants food. Color helps it. The animal cannot see the big cat.

Color helps this little frog, too. Some animals want to eat it, but they cannot see it.

Look at these animal homes. What colors can you see?

mountains

jungle

desert

grasslands

In the mountains

This is a snow leopard.
She lives in the mountains.

The rocks are brown and
black. The snow is white.

snow

fur

The snow leopard's fur is brown, black, and white.

rock——

There is a snow leopard in
this picture. Can you see her?

Ibex live in the mountains, too.

Their fur is orange, and the rocks are orange, too.

Some animals eat ibex.

Can they see the baby ibex
in front of the rocks?

In the jungle

Lots of animals eat insects.

The trees are brown and green. The insects are brown and green, too.

Can you see the insects?

Some geckos live in the jungle. They eat insects.

Color helps them, too.

Geckos can change their color.

Can you see the gecko?

In the desert

This gecko lives in the desert.

sand

It is pink, brown, yellow, orange, black, and white.

What color is the sand?

In the grasslands

This cat lives in the grasslands of Africa.

She can hear a rat.

The brown rat is in the brown grass.

Color helps all these animals.

Activities

The key below describes the skills practiced in each activity.

Spelling and writing

Reading

Speaking

? Critical thinking

Preparation for the Cambridge Young Learners exams

1 Find the words.

coramountainsjoelexjunglewelsondesertinstpadgrasslandssberarockalenssnowpet

mountains
jungle
desert
grasslands
rock
snow

29

2 Look and read. Put a ☑ or a ☒ in the boxes. 📖 ⬡

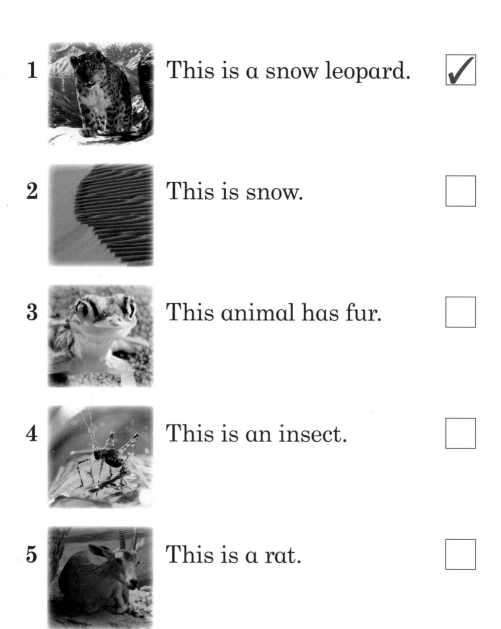

1   This is a snow leopard.   ✓

2   This is snow.

3   This animal has fur.

4   This is an insect.

5   This is a rat.

3 Ask and answer the questions with a friend. 🗨

1  *What colors is this animal?*

This animal is brown, black and white.

2  What colors is this animal?

3  What colors is this animal?

4  What colors is this animal?

4 **Circle the correct words.**

1 Color helps some

   a animals.   **b** sand.

2 This big cat wants

   a food.   **b** friends.

3 Color helps this little _____, too.

   a dog   **b** frog

4 Some animals want to eat it, but they cannot _____ it.

   a look   **b** see

5 **Read the questions.**
Write the answers. 📖 ✏️

1  What colors can you see in the mountains?

brown and white

2  What colors can you see in the jungle?

3  What colors can you see in the desert?

4  What colors can you see in the grasslands?

6 **Read the text. Choose the correct words and write them next to 1—5.**

1	grass	sand	snow
2	in	on	under
3	insects	rocks	trees
4	black	red	white
5	eyes	feet	fur

This is a [1] ___snow___ leopard.

She lives [2] _____ the mountains.

The [3] _____ are brown and

black. The snow is [4] _____.

The snow leopard's [5] _____ is

brown, black, and white.

7 **Read the sentences and match them with the correct animal. Write 1—4.** 📖 ❓

1 This animal lives in the mountains and it has orange fur.

2 This animal lives in the mountains and it has brown, black, and white fur.

3 This animal lives in the jungle and it can change color.

4 This animal lives in the grasslands and it is brown.

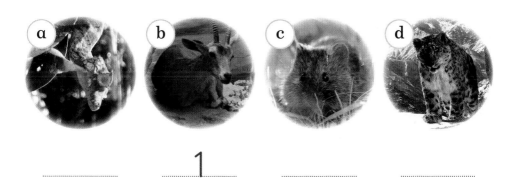

a   b   c   d

1

8 **Look at the letters.**
Write the words. ✏️ ⬡

1 t i c e n s

i n s e c t

2 e x i b

3 s w n o   e l d o r a p

4 a r t

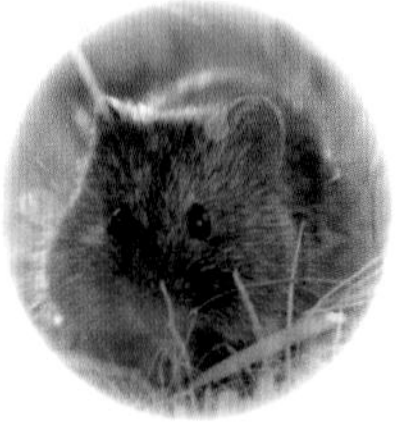

5 k o g e c

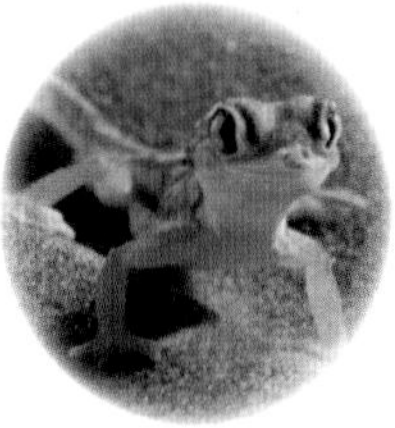

9 Write *are* or *is*.

1 This animal ___is___ an ibex.
Ibex live in the mountains.

2 Their fur _____ orange.

3 The rocks _____ orange, too.

4 Where _____ the baby ibex?

10 **Complete the sentences.**
Write a—d.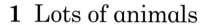

1 Lots of animals ....b........

2 The trees are ....

3 The insects are brown ....

4 Can you ....

a see the insects?

b eat insects.

c brown and green.

d and green, too.

11 Talk about the two pictures with a friend. How are they different? Use the words in the box. ◗

jungle desert tree orange
sand green pink yellow

a

b

In picture a, the gecko lives in the jungle.

In picture b, the gecko lives in the desert.

12 Look at the picture and read the questions. Write the answers.

In the grasslands

This cat lives in the grasslands of Africa.

She can hear a rat.

The brown rat is in the brown grass.

1 Where does this cat live?

In the grasslands of ___Africa___.

2 What can she hear?

She can hear a _____.

3 Where is the rat?

The rat is in the _____.

13 Do the crossword. 📖 ✏️

Across

2 There are a lot of trees here.

5 A snow leopard is a big . . .

6 It is a small animal with brown fur.

7 It is white and cold.

8 It is in the desert, and it is yellow.

Down

1 Geckos eat these.

3 These are on mountains.

4 Grasslands are this color.

14 **Talk with a friend about the pictures. One picture is different. How is it different?** 💬 ❓

1

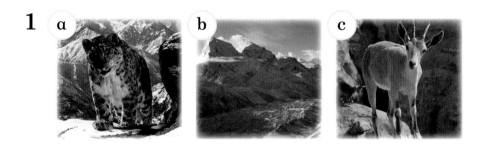

Picture b is different, because you cannot see any animals.

15 **Write the correct questions.**

1 (colors) (the) (snow leopard) (is) (What) (?)

What colors is the snow leopard?

2 (see) (What) (you) (colors) (can) (?)

....

3 (ibex) (the) (Where) (live) (does) (?)

....

4 (see) (baby) (Can) (ibex) (the) (they) (?)

....

5 (does) (eat) (gecko) (a) (What) (?)

....

16 **Circle the correct answers.**

1 Where does the snow leopard live?

　a in the jungle

　(**b** in the mountains)

2 What do lots of animals eat?

　a insects

　b trees

3 Which animal can live in the jungle and in the desert?

　a gecko

　b rat

4 What color is the ibex?

　a green

　b orange

17 Put a ✓ by the animals in this book. 📖 ❓

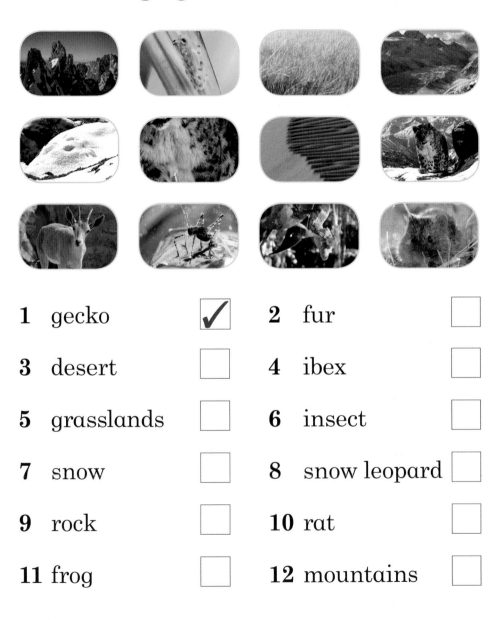

1 gecko	✓	**2** fur		
3 desert		**4** ibex		
5 grasslands		**6** insect		
7 snow		**8** snow leopard		
9 rock		**10** rat		
11 frog		**12** mountains		

18 **Look and read.**
Write *All* or *Some*.

1 _____All_____ animals eat food.

2 _____ animals eat insects.

3 _____ animals have fur.

4 _____ animals have a home.

5 _____ animals live in the jungle.

19 Talk to a friend about animals.

1

> *Do you like animals?*

> *Yes, I do.*

2 Which is your favorite animal?

3 What color is it?

4 Where does it live?

5 What does it eat?

Anansi Helps a Friend 978-0-241-25409-7	**Cinderella** 978-0-241-25407-3	**The Enormous Turnip** 978-0-241-25408-0	**Jon's Football Team** 978-0-241-25411-0	**The Magic Porridge Pot** 978-0-241-25406-6
Rex the Big Dinosaur 978-0-241-29741-4	**Fairy Friends** 978-0-241-28351-6	**Topsy and Tim Go to the Zoo** 978-0-241-25414-1	**Topsy and Tim Go to the Farm** 978-0-241-28355-4	**Topsy and Tim Go to London** 978-0-241-29743-8
On the Farm 978-0-241-25413-4	**Cars** 978-0-241-28354-7	**Peter Rabbit Goes to the Island** 978-0-241-25415-8	**Peter Rabbit and the Radish Robber** 978-0-241-29742-1	**The Tale of Peter Rabbit** 978-0-241-31614-6
In the Garden 978-0-241-26220-7	**Fun with Old Things** 978-0-241-26219-1	**The Fair** 978-0-241-28357-8	**Daddy Pig's Old Chair** 978-0-241-28356-1	**On a Boat** 978-0-241-29744-5
Going Swimming 978-0-241-31613-9	**Going to the Moon** 978-0-241-36544-1	**Pom Pom is Grumpy** 978-0-241-35794-1	**The Birthday Button** 978-0-241-36528-1	**Decepticons in the Scrapyard** 978-0-241-31943-7
Baby Animals 978-0-241-29745-2	**Deserts** 978-0-241-31608-5	**Animal Colors** 978-0-241-35792-7		

Now you're ready for Level 2!